MY AM

Karen Katz

ERICA

GODWINBOOKS

Henry Holt and Company
New York

Henry Holt and Company, *Publishers since 1866*
Henry Holt® is a registered trademark of Macmillan Publishing Group, LLC
120 Broadway, New York, NY 10271
mackids.com

Library of Congress Control Number: 2019950009
ISBN 978-0-8050-9012-3

Our books may be purchased in bulk for promotional, educational, or business use. Please contact
your local bookseller or the Macmillan Corporate and Premium Sales Department at
(800) 221-7945 ext. 5442 or by email at MacmillanSpecialMarkets@macmillan.com.

First edition, 2020 / Book designed by Gene Vosough
The artist used gouache and colored pencils and then collaged to create the illustrations in this book.
Printed in China by RR Donnelley Asia Printing Solutions Ltd., Dongguan City, Guangdong Province

1 3 5 7 9 10 8 6 4 2

To my little bug, Elaina Jane

Children come to live in America from many different

AMER

Some come from far, far away . . . some come from very near. Some

countries. And for many different reasons.

ICA

come on a plane, some come in a car, and some come on a boat.

Some come with moms and dads, and others come with aunts or uncles.

Some come with grandparents, and some come alone.

Some are tiny babies and others have grown big.

They come to make America their new home.

Somalia

Barasho wanaagsan. My name is Faduma.
I was born in Somalia, where it is very hot.
Now I live in Minnesota, where it gets very cold.

Minnesota

We have lots of snow. I love snow!

South Korea

안녕하세요 (ahn-nyeong-hah-seh-yoh).
My name is Tae.
I came to New York City from South Korea
when I was three.
A lot of things are different here.
Especially the food.
In South Korea I ate a lot of rice, soup,
and kimchi.

New York City

I still do, but now I also eat New York–style pizza!

Mexico

Hola (oh-lah). My name is María. When I was five, my aunt and uncle drove me from Mexico to Florida. I didn't know any English. I was very shy. I worked hard to learn. Now I speak English *and* Spanish.

Florida

4

I have so many friends who helped me!

India

नमस्ते (nah-mah-stay).
My name is Samaira.
I came here from India because my
mom got a really good job.
I used to live in a big, noisy city.
Now it is very quiet where I live.

Pennsylvania

I wear a bindi on my forehead.
It's beautiful and means good fortune.

Nepal

नमस्ते (nah-mah-stay).
My name is Nabin.
We came from Nepal to live in Kansas.
In Nepal, my family lived in two rooms.

Kansas

Now I get to have my very own bedroom!

مرحباً (mar-ha-bahn). **My name is Jori.
I came here from Syria with my mom, dad,
and brother.
It was hard to go to school in my country.**

Now we live in Texas and we go to school every day.

Sweden

Hej (hay). My name is Anna.
My dad's great-grandfather and great-grandmother
came on a ship from Sweden in 1895.
They built a small log cabin in Wisconsin.

Wisconsin

All my family lives here . . . uncles, aunts, cousins, nephews, and nieces. We have been here a long time.

Iraq

مرحباً (mar-ha-bahn). **My name is Salim. I came from Iraq. Now I live in California. I've always played soccer, but now I also play baseball.**

California

I'm really good at second base!

Приве́т (pree-vyet).
My name is Stas.
I came from Russia.

Cześć (cheshch).
My name is Marta.
I came from Poland.

Hola (oh-lah).
My name is Lena.
I came from Guatemala.

ሰላም:: (sah-lahm).
My name is Dani.
I came from Ethiopia.

We came here for many different reasons.

I came to be with my family.

I came to have food and shelter.

I came to go to school.

I came to feel safe.

I came for new opportunities.

**This is my new home.
This is . . .**

"Give me your tired, your poor,

Your huddled masses

yearning to breathe free,

The wretched refuse

of your teeming shore.

Send these, the homeless,

tempest-tost to me,

I lift my lamp beside the golden door!"

—Emma Lazarus, from "The New Colossus," written in 1883